MILLICENT'S MISADVENTURES ON BLARGTHON-6

MICKIE SILVER

CONTENTS

MILLICENT PLUCKED HER PIECE

Millicent plucked her piece of toast from the toaster, sat down at her breakfast nook, and prepared to spread a teaspoon of margarine onto its perfectly browned surface.

She considered heading into the pantry to retrieve the marmalade, then shook that wild thought right out of her neurons. Marmalade was a special occasion condiment.

"Millicent," she said to herself. She said it silently, inside her own head. Speaking out loud would have been mad. She was the only one in her household. "You listen here. This is no special occasion. This is Tuesday."

And so Millicent, in her household of one, just finished with a sip of her plain English Breakfast tea, no cream, no sugar, prepared at the ideal temperature (95 degrees Celsius) and with adequate but not overblown steeping time to allocate no more than 22 milligrams of caffeine (3 minutes), glanced down momentarily at her hand to observe the process by which she spread the margarine onto the bread, only to catch sight of a most unsightly lump.

This unsightly lump was on her own forearm.

Protruding from it.

Green.

It had a face.

The face had a mouth.

This unsightly arm lump opened its hideous mouth and squeaked, "Greetings!"

Millicent shrieked. She flung her margarine knife and her toast, and knocked the toast plate onto the floor, and threw over her teacup with such force that it shattered as soon as it hit the ground while on previous days the same accident would cause no more than a clatter, a chip, to be glued into place once spotted on Millicent's newly washed kitchen floor.

The lump was undaunted.

"Greetings!" It proclaimed again. "I will be your guidelump!"

"My guidelump for what?" Millicent said.

"Your guidelump for Blargthon-6," the lump said.

"What's Blargthon-6?" Millicent's voice had evened out quite a bit following her initial shriek. For somebody with a talking lump on her arm, it was conversational.

No sooner had Millicent popped the question than her kitchen wavered, shimmered, and disappeared, to reveal the surface of a planet that did not resemble her kitchen in Bristol in any way.

"This is," her guidelump said.

"I see," Millicent said. "What happened to Blargthons one through five?"

"You must be an accountant," Millicent's guidelump said.

"I am," Millicent said. "How did you know?"

"The only people who asked about the other Blargthons were all accountants," the guidelump said.

"Things have to be accounted for," Millicent said. "Including Blargthons."

The sky was red, streaked with orange and purple, reflected in a vapor that hung on the ground around Millicent's ankles.

Millicent wasn't wearing any shoes, clad instead in a pair of slippers still, as was her custom when she ate breakfast.

She ran a shoes-off household so as to not track crud around the carpet and floors.

The vapor dampened her slippers and soaked in to create a clammy situation for her feet. She shivered, though it wasn't so cold here. Based on her skin reactions, Millicent figured it to be about 20 degrees. But wet feet were the worst.

In the distance, a volcano erupted, belching orange gas into the sky between two suns shrouded by the atmospheric haze.

Millicent turned to look in the other direction, and was mildly surprised to see an other-wordly replica of Bristol County Ground.

"What's that?" Millicent asked her guidelump. The guidelump had been mostly silent while Millicent appraised the situation, with the exception of some vocal hitching that sounded quite a bit like hiccups. "Do you have hiccups?"

"I—*hep*—do," the guidelump said. Its tiny lump body shuddered, a curious feeling on Millicent's arm. She was working hard not to try to pull, pry, or dig at the lumpsite. It seemed rude, counterproductive.

2

"I don't see how," Millicent said. "You can't possibly have a whole throat and respiratory system in there. You're not eating food, are you? And...excreting...it?" Millicent drew this last question out with big swallows between each word, as if she were being made to swallow those excretions. Her brow furrowed.

"Is that a sore spot with you, Millicent? If I were to have shat in your   arm?"

BEFORE MILLICENT COULD RESPOND

Before Millicent could respond, the guidelump changed the subject.

"You asked a question. As your guidelump, I must answer. Promptly and accurately. It's the guidelump way. That is the blargging stadium. It's where most of the blargging happens. Except in special circumstances, when the blargging has to be taken to another site. Very. Special. Circumstances."

The guidelump drew this last sentence out as if the whole sha-bang wasn't a very special circumstance for Millicent.

"So, blargging. You've mentioned it a number of times. What's blargging?"

Before Millicent had really even finished saying blargging, the surface of the planet disappeared, and she was surrounded by the reasonable facsimile of Bristol County Ground she'd spotted from afar. Though there were a few major differences.

The stands were occupied by species that did not look like they were from Bristol, or England, or Earth. They were making general noises, some of which could have been construed as stadium-appropriate hollering. There were also beeps and clicks and whistles, trumpets, and a distinctly didgeridoo-esque noise Millicent recognized only due to a television documentary. She'd never been on any territory other than that of the island of the United Kingdom.

This was her first trip anywhere.

A loudspeaker broadcast some sounds which may have been the common language. Unfortunately, it wasn't English, so Millicent hadn't the faintest idea what the announcement was.

Millicent was dead center in the stadium, as if she were the sporting attraction, something that had never happened to Millicent in her entire life. Hundreds of different kinds of creatures, none of which would have ever occurred to Millicent to exist, were staring at her. Making their sounds. Some gesturing in her direction. Some waving their tentacles at the opposite end of the stadium.

And, something was running at her, a distant bipedal creature. Millicent squinted to make out what it was. She needn't squint for long, because it was gaining distance. Towards her. It was leading with its, was it holding...what was that?

"Just a suggestion," the Guidelump said. "But, you might want to start running too."

It wasn't holding anything.

"Start running where?" Millicent asked, jamming her slippers on to a more secure spot on her feet.

"Oh, you know." The guidelump paused to hiccup again. "Away."

The protrusion was in the middle of the entity's body. If Millicent could trust alien anatomy to be roughly spatially similar to human physiology, and she wasn't sure if she could or couldn't, but if it could, then she was certainly viewing an alien penis.

"You didn't say what blargging is," Millicent said to the Guidelump, taking up a jog at a healthy clip now that she saw her pursuer. She zig-zagged back and forth across the stadium, not at all the greens it would have been back home. Instead, she was slipping around on a purple silt that threatened to skid out from under her, leaving her at the mercy of this—

The only thing more shocking than the creature's general shape was its penis.

Millicent had allowed two penises into her vagina over the course of her 42 years: the first to try it out, and the second to confirm she didn't like it. Wasn't interested. Not feeling the advertised feelings.

If *this* thing got a hold of her, and put *its* thing into her, she'd feel some feelings. For sure. And, predictively speaking, they wouldn't be enjoyable.

It was at least seven feet tall and three feet wide, the creature. It lumbered, and that was the only thing Millicent had going for her. But it was doing a good job of lumbering. It had caught up. Millicent was fatiguing, though the atmosphere was roughly the same as Earth's. Too much time in the cubicle.

She should have let the tea steep a bit longer, for more of a caffeine boost. She would have, if she'd known what was coming. The guidelump. Blargthon-six.

Blargging.

5

THE BLARGTHON HAPPENS ON

"The Blargthon happens on Blargthon-six once every year," the Guidelump said. Its tone was rushed and squeaky. Millicent was certain they were sharing some bodily functions. Which implied the Guidelump *had* shat in her arm and was being withholding about it.

This Guidelump was being withholding about a lot of things.

"What's this thing? How do I get out of here? What happens if it catches up to me?" She feinted right, then ran left. This was the only time Millicent ever wished she had worn her shoes indoors, at the breakfast table. Her house slippers were absolutely dismal for running in alien silt. But her fancy footwork paid off anyway. The alien was thrown off course and just top heavy (penis-heavy) enough to be thrown off balance. It tripped and fell. The crowd roared. Millicent couldn't tell if it was approval or hatred. And whose side were they on?

Probably the penis side. That was an educated guess, based on Earth life.

"Whoa, whoa, whoa," the Guidelump said in its breathy squeak. "One at a time."

Luckily, the creature was having a hard time getting back on its feet-tentacles. It had grazed the side of its penis, the part with the chainsaw-like protrusion, and was writhing in pain.

"I'm not asking again," Millicent shouted at the Guidelump.

At least the Blargthon-sixians felt pain. If they were invincible, Millicent might have a chainsaw alien penis inside her this moment.

Well, it *appeared* to be writhing in pain. What did she know about alien behavior? Millicent sprinted as far away from her adversarial alien as possible, then seized on the Guidelump, and gave it a swift compression with her thumb and her forefinger.

"HEY HEY HEY HEY HEY," the Guidelump said.

"Answers," Millicent said.

"Accountants are vicious," the Guidelump said.

"Only when provoked," Millicent said.

"You should be happier," the Guidelump said. "And more easygoing. You just won this round."

A spaceship hovered overhead. Millicent's reflexes were off here. She hadn't noticed it.

It opened its hatch. Millicent peered into its depths, but couldn't make anything out, it was so dark.

A clump emerged. Another monster?

Party streamers. They landed on the ground next to her in a thud.

"This celebration could have been implemented better," Millicent said. "Now can I go home? I'll be late for work. My tea must be cold by now."

"Spoken like a true accountant," the Guidelump said. "Blargthon-six isn't over just yet."

"I thought that was the planet." Millicent glanced over at the creature. It was still flopping its legs around. Was it even trying to get up? A thick, dark liquid was now dripping out of its gargantuan chainsaw penis. She swiveled her head all around, alert for the next attack.

"It is. The planet. The competition. We reuse words here. We're efficient. You like efficiency, don't you, Millicent?"

Millicent appraised the creature and the motor oil sludge pooling around its protruding shaft and tried to remain neutral about it, pretended it was a column of numbers she had to examine. "So this is a victory for me? How, exactly?"

The Guidelump chuckled its shrill chuckle.

"You won this round of Blargthon-six. Congratulations, Millicent. You're the most successful contestant we've ever hosted."

"It's not hosting if you kidnap the guest. Then it's a kidnapping."

"Oh, Millicent. You're so literal. I don't know how you're ever going to make it here."

"What do you mean, 'make it here'? I have to get to work."

The Guidelump laughed again, this time a long, hearty, low-pitched (based on Millicent's limited lump vocal experience) laugh.

"What are you laughing about? We're done here, aren't we? I don't think he...it's getting up." Millicent peeked back at her adversary, still wriggling in the silt. "I won."

Whatever this was, this 'Blargthon-Six', it wasn't over.

THE CROWD STAYED PUT

The crowd stayed put in the stands. Millicent shielded her eyes from the suns to get a better look. Lots of tentacles out there. Some signs. Most illegible, but on one, there was a crude drawing of a female humanoid stick figure being impaled by the appendage that lay flopped on the ground. Millicent wondered if she should chop it off.

"Am I supposed to kill it?" Millicent asked her Guidelump.

"Oh, heavens, no. That would be ghastly."

"Really? Because there's a sign over there that pretty much depicts the same thing happening to me."

"There you go again. Being literal. It's just a sign. Part of the festivities."

The Guidelump wasn't very helpful, but Millicent decided to take its advice and restrained herself from the more violent tactics. Not just out of courtesy, and because she needed an ally, but because the ground was rumbling.

A massive structure burst up out of the ground. One imperial foot thick, the length and height of half the field. It rose and rose until it towered over them all.

A sphere came whizzing out from behind the stands, crashed into an errant flapping tentacle, fell, recovered, continued to approach at a terrifying pace, stopped just short of Millicent's face. And there it was, broadcast on the screen.

Millicent's face. Cringing for impact. She was quite flushed, she noted.

The morning had been more active than usual.

"Oh," piped the Guidelump. "They must be activating phase 2. That's a good sign."

"What's phase 2?"

A cloud darkened on the horizon, changed in color from pink to green to a deep blue. Millicent wanted to ask about it. Would there be rain? Did Blargthon-six have something more reprehensible than rain? Lava, perhaps? Or an ecosystem composed of alien semen?

Was it part of the game?

"Well, it's tough to explain ahead of time."

"You're supposed to be guiding me. You're a guidelump. Try, why don't you? When somebody brings me a series of disordered financial accounts, I don't just throw up my hands and leave them in the lurch. I work on it."

"Okay, okay. Don't question my fitness for purpose."

"I wouldn't have to if you would answer questions. *Guide*. In fact, I'm not carrying on unless you answer at least three questions."

"Well—"

"What do you mean, well? Here are my questions. What's that cloud on the horizon going to drop on me? What's the purpose of this nonsense? And what's phase 2? How do I get home?"

"You, as an accountant, should be aware that that was five questions, but I am more than appropriately fit to do this job, so I'll answer all of them."

"Great," Millicent said. Her massive image on the screen inspired a twinge of self-consciousness. She didn't look her best, though her appearance most likely wasn't the main attraction to the aliens in the stands. She took the opportunity to straighten her clothes, brush some silt off her slippers, smooth her hair.

"The cloud on the horizon is going to—"

The cloud wasn't on the horizon, though: now it was directly above her, in no time at all.

Before the Guidelump had a chance to expound, to impart even the slightest bit of information about what was going on, why Millicent had been selected for this assignment, what exactly the goal and the quasi-sexual-cum-bloodsport-murdery undertones of her particular situation were leading to, precisely, how she'd gotten there, what was about to transpire, and above all, WHY, why why why, what would have been a most illuminating conversation was interrupted by the cloud itself.

It was more than a cloud, she now saw. Had more shape. A shape that shifted, then solidified.

And then beamed a column down, a column that emitted the most horrific high pitched whine.

The column connected with Millicent's head.

"Oh dear—" was all Millicent managed to utter, before she was entirely   consumed.

5

DARKNESS.
SQUOOISHINESS.

Darkness. Squooshiness. A warm liquid all around her. Including...in her mouth. Wait a second. She didn't have a mouth anymore.

Blast this Blargthon-six.

Millicent barely formed the thought, and when she strained to figure out why, she found herself largely incapable of conceptual thought. In fact, her brain could barely form pictures.

Darkness.

Bouncing.

Millicent looked down, or up, or sideways, she couldn't tell, because of the way she was packaged. She flung her appendages out.

Hit a stretchy membrane.

Periods of consciousness and unconsciousness.

Music. Blaring. Pressed up against her containment sac.

Millicent summoned all her strength, and kicked the membrane. It stretched, but did not break.

"Oof," she heard. The sound of this rumbled all around her, vibrated the liquid cave she was in. A cave with no apparent exit.

Millicent couldn't concoct a whole lot of thinking about this, but just vaguely, somewhere in the back of her brain, an understanding dawned on Millicent.

She was now a fetus.

***

Millicent started out rather small, as fetuses do, and grew up over time. Time was difficult to measure, because there weren't any clocks in the womb, nor any natural light. So she had to go by the rhythms of the creature she inhabited. Periods of extreme turbulence cropped up. She heard muffled noises that could have been talking. Could have been anything though, what did she know about alien civilization?

There was one noise that was consistent. Barely audible. Squeaky. Got louder over time. Until one day, when her appendages had regrown to a considerable size, there was a muffled but noticeable:

"This is my least favorite part of the Blargthon."

"Guidelump?" Millicent tried to say, but she was in a sac of liquid and had an as-yet underdeveloped mouth, throat, and vocal cords. It came out as little more than a glug.

"I know you've got some complaints, all of us do. Mine is the shrinking, the incubation, but most of all—the birthing."

Millicent glugged again. There was no way to communicate and it irked her to no end, so she thrashed and kicked her host. She turned her eyes downwards to what used to be her left arm, now a shrunken and lesser version of itself. The tiniest fleck of green was speaking there on it, even through the viscous liquid that housed them both.

"Take it easy! You want to win, don't you? There's no sense in making enemies before the real trial."

Millicent was so angered by her inability to ask follow-up questions, she tried to use her partially formed appendage to smack at the Guidelump. But she was squished into an awkward position among her host's organs and unable to reach. She tried anyway, reaching and flexing, arching, and glugging, until she fell asleep, exhausted.

Day whatever on Blargthon-six. Millicent's mind had sharpened over the course of her time in the womb. Expanded. She could form whole concepts by now, but at the same time, she could barely remember what life was like before.

Before what?

There it was. Happening again.

Hold onto it, she told herself. Go over what you know.

My name is Millicent.

I'm an accountant in Bristol.

This morning I ate toast and tea for breakfast. This is my typical routine.

I was about to head to work when I found myself transported to what appeared to be another planet.

Oh, but before that, immediately before that, I looked down at my arm to find—

Millicent bowed her head down in the thick goo to see...

The Guidelump.

"Hi!" It piped. "Not long now."

Before what? Millicent thought again.

She had been in this *"Before what?"* loop for a long time, it seemed.

And then there was a howl so thunderous, so rattling, Millicent thought she'd been deafened.

The liquid all around her drained in one splatter.

6
MILLICENT SAW A LIGHT

Millicent saw a light.

A tunnel.

A light at the end of a tunnel.

Now that the liquid was gone, the membrane was right up against her face.

And inside her mouth.

She couldn't breathe.

The magical power of the viscous liquid to somehow provide oxygen was replaced with the practical effect of a membrane suffocating her by sticking to her face.

She punched and kicked, harder and harder.

Nothing.

She wasn't getting anywhere. She was going to lose consciousness. Then what? She made one last effort to push towards the light. The narrow canal pressed her, crushed her head and body, but she had to go, keep burrowing out, going and going, pressing and stretching until—

Millicent landed on the floor, head first, in a mass of liquid, goo, ooze, blood, tissue, some larger and well-organized fleshy clumps that might have been alien organs. She rolled over and looked up, blinking her blinded eyes open. Wiped the goo out with what was now a fully formed human, adult Millicent hand. She tilted her head down, and there was her same old body. Her neck muscles gave out. Everything was a weak and shaky mess. Her head flopped, side to side, eyes coming to rest on the canal from whence she'd erupted, only to glimpse something in motion on the periphery of her visual field.

A large, penile-like appendage standing straight up in the air, with a chainsaw-esque formation at the end.

Millicent scrambled backwards, slipping and sliding in the goo.

"Muh wuh." These were her first post-birth words, once she'd gotten a handle on her first reaction: a little light screaming.

She was actually trying to express a common saying of hers, *my word*, but her vocal cords, lips, and most everything else on her body was atrophied.

Her adversary hadn't changed much since the last she'd seen of him. And, from the looks of things, she'd just been birthed out of his anus.

Millicent struggled to get her bearings. Her physical abilities and thoughts were still impaired, perhaps not as much as those of an actual fetus thrust into the world.

Except Millicent was an adult with a full 41 years on Earth prior to this complex birthed moment. So she was experiencing a full return of her Earth memories, a return of her Blargthon-Six memories, along with a fetus-like struggle to use her arms and legs and senses and brain.

Millicent re-discovered her Guidelump. "Ha la warthar?" She asked. It wasn't quite adequate as an expression of language, but she decided the Guidelump ought to be able to translate. What was a Guidelump for, anyway, if not able to extrapolate the meaning behind some garbled mumbling of its only charge? The Guidelump looked a bit stunned itself, tiny lump mouth open, lumpiness askew rather than plumply spherical in shape, as when they first met, and its vibrant green color now paled.

But it understood.

"Nine months," it piped. "Nine stinking, goopy months for you and me both, lady." It spat a bit of afterbirth up and onto her arm.

"Blarg?" Was all Millicent managed.

"Oh, it's still going. Look, I know I could have been a little more timely with information, and I'm working on it. So here it is. You'd better get your legs working, get your act together, and run."

"Flah?"

Millicent scrambled to get her legs under her, but there was goo all about. She slipped and slid her legs around and around, yet got nowhere.

Her opponent was stirring. Grunting. Millicent still had some abdominal strength in her despite nine months in the anal womb of an alien, so she inched and scrunched her way across the room, then peered back.

The effort of turning her head nearly did her in. Its limbs were twitching.

She scrunched and wriggled faster, out the open door.
Its   grunt   echoed   into   the   hallway.

7

MILLICENT'S RIGHT ARM GAINED

Millicent's right arm gained the slightest bit of strength, transitioned from mere flop to near-heft capacity, so she could slide herself on her alien uterine goo down the hall and away from the birth site.

She slid bit by bit past a window to the outside. From her vantage point on the cold metallic floor, she couldn't view the full scene, but the uppermost levels of the replica of Bristol County Ground were visible, still packed with spectators, and a floating screen on the left, on which she was sliding herself down a lengthy metal hallway. Bit by bit.

And on the far right end of the screen, a chainsaw-esque appendage edged into the shot.

There it was. It? Him? Her? Did Blargthon-6 have gender?

"Is that really what we're going to concentrate on here?" The Guidelump shrieked.

"You can read my thoughts!" Millicent intoned in the depths of her brain. "You could read my thoughts the whole time and you were just choosing to ignore them, you traitor."

"I don't know if gender is really the most focus-worthy thing we've got going on here!" The Guidelump bellowed. "Run! Run, damn you!"

"You could read my thoughts this entire time?" Millicent shrieked back. Then she vomited a loud splat's worth of uterine goo onto the floor. She grabbed the window sill and an inexplicable spike that jutted out of the wall and heaved herself up.

"Garrrrrrr," the creature called. Millicent paused and looked at it. Was it lovingly looking at her? She couldn't be certain. Maybe nine months in the womb had fooled her brain into thinking she could interpret the alien mind of a Blargthon-6 assassin.

Millicent took a cautious step. She was still so slippery. Running wasn't going to be an option.

"What are you waiting for?" The Guidelump said. "Hurry up!"

"I don't even know what the danger is, though," Millicent said. "I mean, we just spent nine months together. What's the problem? Maybe we're friends now."

"Garrrrr," the creature's three mouths parted, tendrils emerged from the left mouth and reached for Millicent. It wasn't moving fast, but it was advancing. Millicent took another step, but this time her leg nearly buckled.

"Blargging isn't about friendship," the Guidelump said. "It's a competition."

"Oh?" A bit of spittle dripped from the corner of the top mouth. "And how do you win? Or I should say, how do I win?"

"I can tell you how he wins," the Guidelump said. "Gratification."

"Gratification?"

"Getting its rocks off," the Guidelump said. "Is that how you say it in Bristol?"

"My word," Millicent said.

"Completion. You get my meaning?"

"How archaic."

"Garrrrr," it said again. It was halfway there. Inching its way forward despite its heft, its slime, its anus blown out since Millicent's birth. It smelled like a bad Tesco cod Millicent had once purchased and had to return.

Millicent looked for a way to continue sliding down the hallway, but there was nothing else to grab to advance her position.

"But what do you mean, completion? It...evacuated me."

"The next step in fetus play," the Guidelump said, "Is ingestion."

"Ingestion? Of what?"

"Of you, Millicent, you ridiculous twat. Of you!"

"Well there's no need to be crass in your warnings," Millicent said. Her opponent was upon her now. Millicent still wasn't in her right mind from the birthing process, or being transported to Blargthon-6 instead of adding and subtracted rows and rows of beautiful numbers, or she wouldn't have done what happened next.

Face to tip with the chainsaw, she noticed a reddened knob on its underside. So she reached out and grabbed it.

The creature bellowed, sucked its tendrils and mouths into its body until it was nearly inside out, rolled into a ball and whirled back into the birthing room.

"Holy shit, Millicent! How the hell did you know to do that?" The Guidelumps eyes were so wide in its lump body that it looked like a series of craters.

"I...didn't," Millicent said. "Have I won the Blargthon now?"

8

THE CROWD OUTSIDE WAS

The crowd outside was going wild, in only the way a multitude of alien species can. Tentacles were falling off, nitrous clouds were shooting from eye tubes, excrement was everywhere.

"Oh dear," Millicent said. "I haven't seen emotions this raw since tax season."

And the hallway disappeared.

The goo disappeared, the metallic hall, the smells, the chill. All gone. Now Millicent was in a room she didn't recognize, though it had an odd familiarity.

The Dorchester. That's what it was. In one of her only trips to London as a child, she and her family had stayed at the Dorchester for one night.

"Don't touch anything," Her father had said. "Or we'll have to pay extra."

Young Millicent, filled with dread at the prospect of paying extra for something though she was years and years away from having any real concept of money, working, payment, or 'extra', touched nothing, and even slept on top of the covers in her adjacent twin bed in the suite.

Now Millicent sat on a massive bed in the Dorchester. The suite wasn't the same but she was sure of it. She got up and clutched one arm, then startled, and gasped: there was no Guidelump there, at all.

'I've lost my mind," Millicent said out loud.

"No you haven't," a deep voice said from the shadows.

"Tony Blair?" Millicent said.

"Yes Millicent, it's me. I took some time off my charitable literacy work just to meet with you. I have a number of accounting questions I'd like to discuss with you."

"Accounting questions? You want to discuss? With me?"

"That's exactly what I said, Millicent. Exactly."

Tony Blair crossed the room to take Milicent's hand and led her back to the bed. He sat, and then patted the bed. And then tugged Millicent down gently next to him.

Gently, but firmly.

Tony Blair wasn't taking no for an answer.

"Alright, sir. What's your question?"

"I notice you looking at me Millicent, and I believe you find me very attractive."

"*Very* is a strong word, sir. I have thought you were attractive at various times in your public service." Millicent blushed and looked away. Tony Blair picked her chin up slightly, and moved in as if to kiss her.

Millicent was appalled and pulled back.

"Millicent, I saw you briefly at a referendum some years ago. I noticed you noticing me, and I've been taken with you ever since."

Tony Blair removed Millicent's outer sweater, her skirt, her leggings, and her undergarments on the lower part of her body.

"Millicent, may I insert my penis in you?"

"Nobody's ever asked my consent in such a specific way," Millicent said. "I suppose. Make sure you wear a condom."

Tony Blair threw off his pants. Millicent was shocked by his total absence of undergarments, which she wouldn't have imagined of a Prime Minister, former or not, but then again, she'd never imagined an undergarment situation at all.

Millicent couldn't believe she was viewing the appendage of the man who had at one time controlled the United Kingdom. She lay back on top of the covers of the bed at Dorchester, much as she had as a child, except this time she was naked from the waist down and consenting to intercourse for the third time in her life, this time with a world leader.

After he rolled the condom over his modest sheath and inserted it into her, he said, "Uhhh, do you like that Millicent?"

"Like is a strong word, sir," Millicent said. "I'm tolerating it for the sake of the experience. It's neither pleasant nor unpleasant."

After a few thrusts, Tony Blair seemed to have had enough. Millicent couldn't tell if he had gotten to completion, as the Guidelump would say, but he--

Wait a second.

Guidelump.

What was a Guidelump? What the hell was happening?

Was Millicent having sex with Tony Blair instead of accounting at   her   office   in   Bristol   today?

9

OR WAS SHE ON

Or was she on an alien planet?

"Sir! You had a question?"

"Eh, sure, yes. My question. It's about the form 990."

"Form 990? Why, that makes no sense. It's an American non-profit tax form, Mr. Prime Minister. We don't use that here in the United Kingdom."

"Well, uh, blarg—I mean, of course."

"Excuse me? Did you just say blarg?"

"No. No, I didn't. Of course not. *Blargthon*!" Tony Blair's face was doing an interesting thing that Millicent could only describe as shimmering.

Then his hand fell off, and a tentacle flopped out.

Millicent leapt up off the bed, which disappeared. Everything disappeared, including the body of Tony Blair, and a many-tentacled monster stood in its place. One of its tentacles was firmly jammed in Millicent's ear. She ripped it out, apparently with a little too much force, because it tore away from the creature's body, too. With the other end dislodged from her inner ear, the rest of the vision vanished.

A motor-oil-like substance drained from the creature-formerly-perceived-as-Tony Blair's-tentacle hole.

It screamed. Millicent screamed. The Guidelump screamed.

Everybody screamed and screamed.

Finally the creature stopped. Millicent stopped. The Guidelump kept on for awhile longer, until it too fell exhausted and stopped.

"Millicent," the Guidelump said.

"What?" Millicent whispered.

"You won the Blargthon."

"I did *what*?"

"You won the Blargthon. You won it. This has never happened before. This is so different from the...others."

"What do you mean? What happened to the others? What happens now, to me?"

"You're going to find out, I suppose. We've never had this particular situation before."

"Why is it that you're supposing and not actually knowing anything? Are you a real Guidelump?"

"How dare you, Millicent. Of course I'm a real Guidelump. I'm meant to guide, not to tell you every single blinking thing in the known Blargosphere. We're learning together, here."

"And this tentacled chap?"

"Oh, Tony Blair?"

"That's rather rude and fraudulent of you to say," Millicent said. "And I don't know how this fellow knew I at one time was attracted to Tony Blair." Millicent lightly tapped the severed tentacle with the toe of her slipper.

"It uplinked to your mind to reveal your deepest, darkest sexual fantasy," the Guidelump said.

"Those were dark times. I was trying to conform to UK standards."

"But then, nothing. As they say, you're dry as a Blyxinsherf in the seventeenth planetary winter."

"I won because I'm not interested in sex?"

"You won the blargging competition. It's totally different. It's not about reproduction. Or attraction. Or desire."

"*Totally* different? I don't know about that. It seems the same as sex to me," Millicent said. "And according to that last experience, equally dull and unsatisfying."

"Maybe he didn't get the tentacle into your brain far enough."

Millicent shrugged. "Can't say a tentacle coming from any creature has ever gotten me over-egged."

"Well, what does get you over-egged, Millicent? If you can't get excited about being transported to an alien planet and blargged by all the greats Blargthon-6 has to offer, what can you get excited about?"

"Numbers," Millicent said.

"Numbers?" the Guidelump echoed, lumpy eyes wide.

"Numbers," Millicent nodded.

"But you can't rail numbers, Millicent. Well, if I'm being honest, and If I understand anything about humans, or independently mobile creatures in general, I suppose numbers can rail you."

"Not getting railed by them, necessarily. Just the numbers. All by themselves. I don't have to insert anything into my body to enjoy it.

They're a concept. That's what I like." Millicent gazed out the window at the purple sky. "I like a good concept. Well. Do I get to return home now? The office will be wondering about me. How long have I been here?"

"Not quite yet," the Guidelump said. "We have to do the ceremony."

***

Millicent entered the grand hall of Blargthon-6 wearing a full suit of what looked, felt, and tasted like candy floss. Her new handlers had insisted, and she didn't know how to communicate *no*. This planet didn't respect free will or wishes or boundaries anyway.

She pulled off a tip of the sleeve and popped it in her mouth, chewed, and swallowed.

"Millicent," the Guidelump said. "Don't eat your victory suit."

10
"I'M FAMISHED."

"I'm famished," Millicent said. "I don't think I've eaten since I was forced into fetushood."

"We'll be eating soon enough," the Guidelump said. "It's all part of your celebration."

The grand metal doors plodded open, pushed by two six-foot-tall slugs. Millicent steadied herself on the trail of slime.

Something that looked like a humanoid poppy flower got right up into Millicent's face, inches away, would have been closer had it not been for the bulk and density of Millicent's victory suit, and then erupted all its pollen right onto Millicent's face, neck, and décolletage.

"That's a very high honor," the Guidelump said.

Millicent squinted to make out who stood at the front of the room. She continued on down the purple carpet, getting stopped here and there by some alien species that wanted to put its two cents in.

"This ceremony wasn't designed for introverts," Millicent murmured.

She could see now who it was at the front of the room: Tentacle Tony Blair.

***

Millicent made it to the front after getting blasted in the face five more times by that many creatures. Or were they species? Did that even exist here? Species? Millicent had been trying so hard not to get fucked on this planet that she didn't even know anything about it.

"Species isn't really the right word," the Guidelump said. "We're not all riding on and made out of the same lump of clay around here like you Earth creatures." The Guidelump had a squeak on the edge of its vocal register that let Millicent know it had been hurt by her implied judgement on its guiding abilities.

And then she was face to tentacles with Tentacle Tony Blair.

"You don't have to refer to me as Tentacle Tony Blair, Millicent," Tentacle Tony Blair said. "I am the Tony Blair, after all."

"What? How did you know I was—" *Thinking that.*

Millicent whirled to disconnect herself from an errant tentacle that Tentacle Tony Blair had slipped into her mind.

He chuckled.

"I bet Mrs. Blair never enjoyed that either," Millicent said.

"Now, now. Just because the ol' Tony Blair tentacle doesn't get you all gobsmacked doesn't mean the missus doesn't love it when I butter her biscuits."

Millicent cringed.

"Fine, fine. Now do I get to go home?"

Tentacle Tony Blair hung a slimy necklace around Millicent's head and left shoulder. The hall erupted, just erupted. Noise, offal, some creature blasted its own head away from its body.

"We've never had a winner before, Millicent!" The Guidelump shrieked above the fracas.

"Oh dear," Millicent said. "Does that mean...?"

"Right. We've never looked into sending anybody back."

"My word."

"But we're going to do whatever we can to keep you happy while we work on figuring that out," Tentacle Tony Blair said. "This is as important to me as my charity work in children's literacy in the UK."

"Oh, well you travel back and forth to the UK, then. How do you get there?"

"I'm a bit of a hologram on the Earth, I'm afraid. A projection."

"I see," Millicent said. She really didn't, though. All those years she had watched Tony Blair on the telly and the internet he'd looked solid enough. But he didn't seem to have tentacles then either.

"But we know what you like now, Millicent." Tentacle Tony Blair yanked on a massive door handle behind them. "And we've got something for you."

"How's that?" Millicent said.

"A surprise," he said.

"You're gonna love it," Guidelump piped.

The doors swung open to reveal lists and lists and lists of numbers.

"Blargthon-6 is in a terrible fiscal crisis," Tentacle Tony Blair shouted.

"Doesn't add up," Guidelump screamed.

A cavernous hallway full of numbers.

Trapped on an alien planet. Would Millicent ever see her kitchen again? What was the office going to do without her? She was their lone accountant.

Lists and lists of numbers.

Deep within her, something inside Millicent stirred.

"Don't worry, Millicent! We'll get you home someday."

MAYBE THIS IS HOME

"Maybe this is home now," Millicent murmured.

Millicent eased into the room and leafed through a few pages, flipping her way through the ends of long and otherwise hideous lime green scrolls that wouldn't have caught her interest in the slightest. Except for the columns and columns of numbers.

Millicent ran her fingers over them. Some looked like the numerical shapes of home, indistinguishable from the books at her office in Bristol, but others were new: an arc here, a spiral with a few adjacent dots there.

She'd have to decipher the patterns to figure out what they all meant. She felt around her ears to make sure Tentacle Tony Blair wasn't manipulating her mind.

But no: this was pure professional numerical interest at work.

Would Millicent stay even if they could safely return her home?

Maybe they could return her home, and were just pretending not to, to take advantage of her accounting skills.

"Nah," the Guidelump said. "We're not great liars, like Earth folks. We're pretty face value, shoot-from-the-hip types."

"Oh really? Because earlier this one—," Millicent jabbed her thumb in Tentacle Tony Blair's general direction, "—stuck his tentacle into my brain to make me think I was back in Bristol and having an affair with the former Prime Minister of the United Kingdom."

"He really was the Prime Minister though," the Guidelump squeaked, "So, that wasn't a lie."

"Well, in that case it was a lie to the entirety of the UK," Millicent said. "Foreigners aren't eligible to become PMs."

"But he was born on UK soil, Millicent."

Tentacle Tony Blair coughed so loudly and intrusively that Millicent and the Guidelump could exchange words no more. After they fell silent, he said, "We were hoping you would enjoy it here. And if you can help us with this fiscal crisis, that would be great."

Millicent caught her breath and set the pages down. She'd upset the balance of a heap of thousands of scrolls. One at the top came loose to tumble down and rest at her feet. She had to turn her back on the whole jumble, she knew, or soon she'd find herself carefully exploring each numerical set. "What fiscal crisis?"

"If we don't get solvent in the next rotation, they're gonna dissolve us." Tentacle Tony Blair's tentacles shriveled a tad when he said, *dissolve.*

"What do you mean, dissolve you? Like a corporation?"

"No, Millicent," the Guidelump piped. "Like sugar in a nice cup of Earl Grey. But with painful fire lasers. And explodey."

Tentacle Tony Blair flared out the ends of several of his tentacles to simulate their collective bodies and planet bursting.

"When does the next rotation end?"

The Guidelump and Tentacle Tony Blair looked at each other.

"Eh," the Guidelump said.

"You see..." Tentacle Tony Blair started, and then trailed off, tentacles sagged, looking at the floor.

"Well?"

"About a week," the Guidelump's squeaky voice broke.

"Excuse me?"

"Uh...a week, Millicent," Tentacle Tony Blair confirmed, still staring hard at the floor.

"What the *sot* are we doing playing this ridiculous competitive sex game when we're about to be liquified?" Millicent kicked a few of the scrolls nearest to her for emphasis.

"Well, we were gonna make some money from the merchandising after you...you know, got it."

"Got what, exactly?"

"Got pulverized in the Blargthon," the Guidelump chirped. "Nothing personal."

"No, of course not," Millicent whispered, in a breathy rage.

Tentacle Tony Blair made a chopping motion with the tips of four of his tentacles.

"Why's everybody acting so blasted happy, then, if we're all about to pop off?" Millicent put her hands on her candy floss-coated hips.

"I didn't tell them," Tentacle Tony Blair said. "You know how I hate to be the bearer of bad news."

"What are you talking about? You delivered nothing but bad news the entire time you were Prime Minister!"

"He waited until after the Blargthon. Then he told them you were a great accountant and you were going to balance the books, solve our fiscal crisis. Otherwise they would have torn you to nanoshreds."

"Well, I *am* a great accountant. That part is true."

"So?" The Guidelump heaved its body towards the fallacious planetary accounts. "Will you give it a go, Millicent?"

"I'll try," Millicent said. "I can't promise anything."

A shadow cast over the room, then stretched across the celebratory hall beyond them, casting a pall so deep and dark, it may have very well stretched across the entirety of Blargthon-6.

"Uh-oh," Tentacle Tony Blair said.

"What's that?" Millicent dropped the few scrolls she'd managed to collect and rushed to the window. A massive gleaming disk floated across the horizon until it blotted out first one and then both suns. A panel opened on its gigantic underbelly, and a spaceship emerged.

"Bill collectors," the Guidelump said.

The ship's rockets expelled a wicked-looking vapor, and then headed directly towards them.

***

Will Millicent save Blargthon-6 from liquidation or get totally obliterated along with the planet and its denizens?

Can she ever return to Earth?

Is Millicent destined to forever have a Guidelump embedded in her arm, and if so, is it shitting in there, and if so, *what happens to that shit*?

Click your way through spacetime and into the next exciting Millicent experience...

MMoB-6 No.2

Millicent Gets Elected the Ruler of Blargthon-Six Due to a Voting Glitch

mickiesilver.com

www.ingramcontent.com/pod-product-compliance
Lightning Source LLC
Chambersburg PA
CBHW071229130626
46555CB00004B/1904